Just Like You

Jo Loring-Fisher

I've got two eyes.

I've got two ears.

I've got one mouth.

And one nose.

I've got
two hands,

two feet,

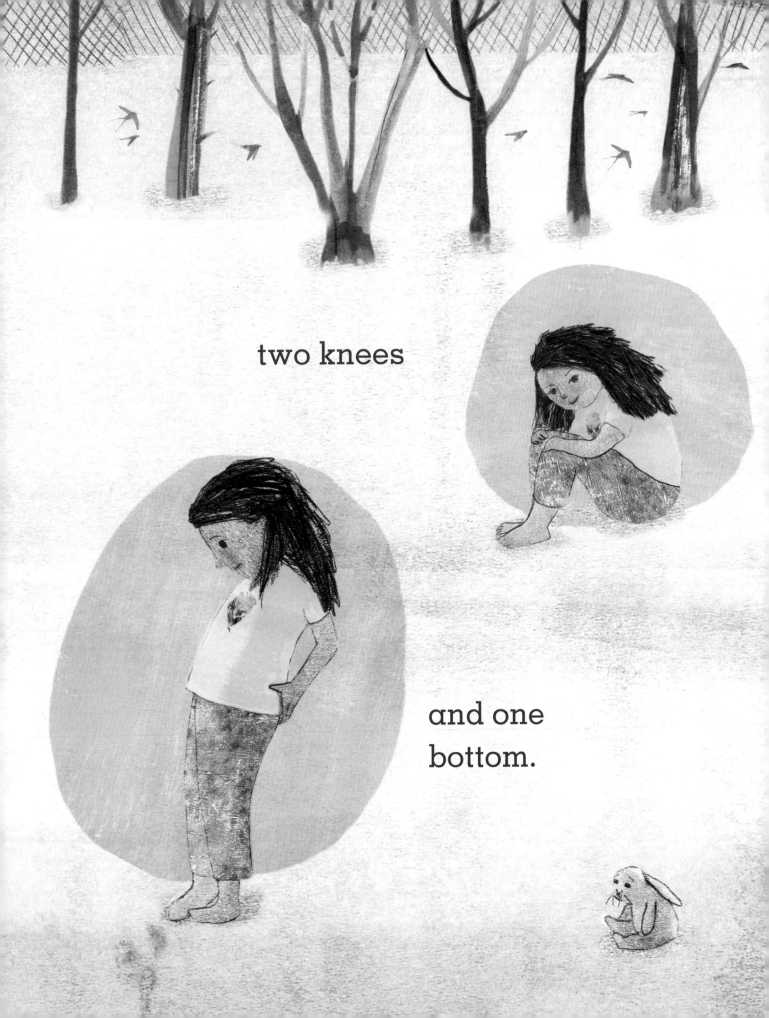

two knees

and one
bottom.

My feet can take me
a long, long way.

They can help me run fast too.

Sometimes
I am very happy.

And at other times, so sad.

But when I'm cuddled
I feel cosy.

And when I'm safe
and warm, I dream.

Just like you.

I am just like you.